TALES FROM THE LAND OF Ooo

by Max Brallier illustrated by Stephen Reed

PSS!
PRICE STERN SLOAN
An Imprint of Penguin Group (USA) Inc.

PRICE STERN SLOAN

Published by the Penguin Group

Penguin Group (USA) Inc., 375 Hudson Street, New York, New York 10014, USA

Penguin Group (Canada), 90 Eglinton Avenue East, Suite 700,
Toronto, Ontario M4P 2Y3, Canada
(a division of Pearson Penguin Canada Inc.)

Penguin Books Ltd, 80 Strand, London WC2R ORL, England

Penguin Ireland, 25 St Stephen's Green, Dublin 2, Ireland
(a division of Penguin Books Ltd)

Penguin Group (Australia), 707 Collins Street,
Melbourne, Victoria 3008, Australia
(a division of Pearson Australia Group Pty Ltd)

Penguin Books India Pvt Ltd, 11 Community Centre,
Panchsheel Park, New Delhi—110 017, India

Penguin Group (NZ), 67 Apollo Drive, Rosedale, Auckland 0632, New Zealand
(a division of Pearson New Zealand Ltd)

Penguin Books, Rosebank Office Park, 181 Jan Smuts Avenue,
Parktown North 2193, South Africa

Penguin China, B7 Jaiming Center, 27 East Third Ring Road North,
Chaoyang District, Beijing 100020, China

Penguin Books Ltd, Registered Offices: 80 Strand, London WC2R ORL, England

ADVENTURE TIME, CARTOON NETWORK, the logos, and all related characters and elements are
trademarks of and © Cartoon Network. (s13)

Published in 2013 by Price Stern Sloan, a division of Penguin Young Readers Group, 345 Hudson Street,
New York, New York 10014. PSS! is a registered trademark of Penguin Group (USA) Inc.
Manufactured in China.

ISBN 978-0-8431-7270-6   10 9 8 7 6 5 4 3 2 1

BONE APPÉTIT

"The Boneyard Kingdom creeps me out majorly," Finn said. "Of all the Kingdoms, Boneyard is def the creepiest."

Finn and Jake were crossing through the dark and horrible Boneyard Kingdom, which is why—y'know—the overwhelming creepiness of the place was on Finn's mind.

The moon cast twisted and misshapen shadows, while tall, spindly trees reached out of the ground like skeletal hands—talons that might grab you at any moment.

It was totes scary.

"Agreed, bro—" Jake began to say, but was stopped short by a sound—a horrible, profane, otherworldly sound that went a lil' something like: *GREEOOOOAARHHHHH!!!*

"Holy demon butts!" Finn exclaimed.

"Sorry, dude," Jake said. "False alarm. That was just my belly." Jake then punched himself in the belly and shouted, "SHUT UP, YELLOW BELLY!"

"Whoa, man, your stomach is *heated*," said Finn.

"Yeah. I'm superstarved," Jake replied. "Where's that snail that's always hanging around? If I saw him, I'd be all like, *nom nom nom*!"

Finn put away his sword, Jake suppressed his hunger, and the two righteous buds continued their trek through the murky woods. Then Finn slowed and squinted. He saw something moving up ahead in the mist.

Suddenly a skeletal figure burst through the haze and said, "Hey, guys!"

"Ahhh!" Finn screamed.

"Sorry!" the skeleton said. "I didn't mean to scare you. I'm Ted."

"No worries, Skeleton Ted," Jake said. "You didn't scare us. *Nothing* scares us. Finn and I were just . . . um . . . playing dentist. Right, Finn?"

"Huh?" Finn said, confused. "Oh, *right*, playing dentist. Yeah. Now it's your turn, Jake. Say *ahh*."

"*Ahhhh!*" Jake said.

"You guys are pretty good at playing dentist!" Skeleton Ted said.

Jake leaned over and whispered to Finn, "Wow, Skeleton Ted totally fell for our playing-dentist ruse."

"In addition to your pearly white teeth, you two look superhealthy," Ted continued, looking the two heroes up and down. "And skinny."

Jake and Finn exchanged glances that said, "This Skeleton Ted is a weirdo bajeerdo, and it'd be nice if he'd stop looking us up and down like that."

"Why don't you come join me and my skeleton pals for dinner?" Skeleton Ted asked, reaching out and taking Finn's hand. "We'd all *love* to have you for dinner."

Finn yanked his hand away. "Whoa, Skeleton Ted, personal space violation! Stop touching me with your weird cold bone hands," Finn said. "We just met. And, um, no thanks on the dinner invite."

But Jake was psyched and already set on a bone meal. "But, dude! I'm *soooo* hungry. C'mon, least we can do is *see* what they're cooking up!"

"*Jake!*" Finn whispered. "You *know* I don't like skeleton dudes."

"Don't be a skeleton hater!" Jake whispered back. "Someday *you'll* be a skeleton!"

"No, l won't!" Finn yelled. "l will never, ever, ever—Oh, wait, l will . . ."

So as Finn contemplated life, death, and the unavoidable fact that someday his heroic heart would stop beating, his fleshy skin would molt away, and he'd turn 100 percent skeleton, Jake took him by the wrist and together the two pals followed Skeleton Ted through the woods of the Boneyard Kingdom.

The moon was high and bright as they came upon a small graveyard. At the center was a long dining table made entirely of bones. The table legs were femurs, and the surface was an intricate interweaving of ribs and finger bones and toe bones and nose bones. Positioned around the table—as chairs—were headstones.

Just beyond the table was a small cottage. Smoke came from the chimney, and it smelled, Jake thought, like some delish down-home skeleton cooking.

Finn and Jake sat together at the head of the table. Skeleton Waiter came out of the cottage wearing bright white waiter gear over his bony figure and said to Finn and Jake, "I am most delighted to be *serving you*."

"Thanks, Skeleton Waiter," Jake said, grabbing handfuls of food and shoving them in his mouth.

"Did you hear that?" Finn whispered to Jake. "He said *serving you*."

"Yeah, bro, that's what waiters do," Jake said between bites. "Jeez. We gotta get you out more."

"*I know what waiters do!* But that monster maître d' made it sound like he was going to be serving us! Like *serving US*. I think we're on the menu! Skin salads or something, dude!"

"Chill out and dig in, buddy," Jake said, jamming more food into his mouth. "Wait! Dude, I *just* got that! *Shoveling* food means you're *digging* in. Like shovels dig? In the earth? What a meal, man. We're eating exotic cuisine *and* catching knowledge."

Finn sighed and reached for an appetizer. But when he saw what it was, he just about vommed. "There's no meat on these bones! These are just, like, *bones*."

"Oh, just eat it, man. You don't want to offend our hosts," Jake said, sucking sloppily on a bone. "Besides, this is primo bone."

Just then, Skeleton Chef came out of the cottage. He stood at the end of the table and announced to Jake, Finn, and the rest of the skeleton gang, "I am proud to reveal the main course. For dinner, I shall be serving . . ."

Everyone waited with bated breath. Well, the two guys that breathed at least: Finn and Jake.

"A couple of meatballs! And from the looks of them, they are going to be *quite delicious*," Skeleton Chef said, staring directly at Finn and Jake through hollow coal-black eye sockets.

"I have a bad feeling about—" Finn started.

"MEATBALLS?" Jake shrieked. "I *looooooooove* meatballs. I am beyond pumped to participate in this skeletal meatball meal."

"*Jake!*" Finn whispered. "*We're* a couple of meatballs! I'm telling you—any second, they're gonna cook us up, dude!"

"Oh, stop being so suspicious and crazy. Here, try a mozzarella finger bone."

"No!" Finn said, slapping away the cheesy metacarpal. "If I'm crazy, then why are those guys staring at us like that?"

"What guys?"

"Dude, *THOSE GUYS*!"

"Oh," Jake said. "They probably just think we're awesome and wanna be like us, so they're watching us carefully and closely so they can study us and stuff."

"Hmm . . . ," Finn said, thinking. "That does make sense."

"Flippin'-A right it does," Jake said, reaching for another bone.

Finn shook his head. "But no. No! I'm telling you, we need to get out of here, like, right now, yesterday time."

"Shh, shh," Jake said, hushing Finn. "Look, Skeleton Waiter is coming. I think it's time for the main course!"

Finn looked up to see Skeleton Waiter stepping out of the small cottage. "Fellow skeletons, it is now time for the main course. I hope you're all ready to eat . . . OUR TWO HEROES!"

"*Ahhh!* That's IT!" Finn yelled. He reached over, slapped the bone out of Jake's mouth, and sent Jake sprawling to the ground.

"We are OUT OF HERE! Serving us! Two meatballs! Eating two heroes. They are one hundred percent talking about us, dude! I flippin' told you!"

"Oh man!" Jake said. "Stupid hunger pangs manipulated my judgment again!"

"I'll bust your chops," Finn said, grabbing Jake.

The duo sprinted into the woods, running as fast as they could.

Back at the table, a single tear dropped from Skeleton Chef's eye socket as he lifted the lid off his serving platter, revealing two piping-hot meatball hoagies.

"I guess they didn't want to try these two delicious meatball heroes . . ."

THE END!

AN EXCERPT FROM
I WROTE ANOTHER BOOK!
BY LUMPY SPACE
PRINCESS

To my LUMPS. I owe all my fabulous success to them.

Hi, gals and pals! Thanks for *reading*. My book editor—who is not all that lumping great—said my last book, *I Wrote a Book* (buy it today!!!) lacked "meaningful content." I don't even know what that LUMPING MEANS, but whatevs.

So this stupid editor was all like, "We're going to release a little part of your next book early (that little part is called an *excerpt*) to whet people's appetites for the whole book."

And I was all like, "Well, if you want to whet their LUMPING appetites, just put more pics of my *smokin' lumps* on the cover!"

Anyway, I'm going to pack a ton of *awesome* stuff into this chapter, so it can be excerpted in *The Lumpy Spacer* magazine, which is, like, super highbrow and talks about plays and stuff, which of course I love because plays=DRAMA!

So . . .

Once upon a time there was a beautiful lumpy space princess . . . me!

I live in this superawesome amazing home. Oh my glob, isn't it just *to die*? I know.

Me in my awesome apartment!
I'm superindependent.
BTLW, this is NOT a
Hobo Camp!

Currently I'm in, like, negotiations to have my beautiful home featured in an episode of *House Finders: Land of Ooo Edition*.

Sometimes Finn and Jake come by. We're besties, even though sometimes Jake calls me a hobo, and I'm all like, "Oh my glob! SHUT YOUR FACE, JAKE! I AM *NOT* A HOBO!"

Now you're probably all, "OMG, LSP, you are

so young and gorge *and* you live on your own in a mansion?!?" EDITOR'S NOTE: It's a hobo mansion.

Well, *yes*. That is all true. I am young and gorge and I live on my own in a mansion. EDITOR'S NOTE: Still a hobo mansion.

There was a whole reason I ended up here on my own, but it's way complicated. Basically I got in a big fight with my stupid mom and dad, and also things were getting soooo dramafied with Brad.

If you've been living under, like, a lumping rock or something, Brad is my stupid ex-BF who I used to eat chili cheese fries with.

My ex-BF, Brad. I dumped him because he got super kissy-kissy. A princess does NOT kiss until a princess is ready to kiss. Your loss, Bradley!

Secretly, I would maybe, possibly, probably, not sure, but kinda definitely take Brad back if he was interested. But I'm sure he's lumping not because he's all lumping intimidated by me and MY LUMPS! GAH! *My beauty is my curse!*

But FYI, babes, being a Lumpy Space Princess is NOT just all riding around in cars with boys and eating beans from a can and looking lumping fabulous. There are downsides. Like, who can you trust in this lumping world? It's TOTALLY "mo lumps, mo problems" out here on the streets.

LSP FACT! My parents are horrible idiots

Melissa is my best friend, but in my celly she is labeled as Best Friend #66 because I don't want her thinking she's all high-and-lumping-mighty.

Ugh, hold on. My celly is blowing up like it's preggers.

"Hello? LSP here. Oh, hiiii, Melissa."

It's *lumping Melissa.* Yes, she's my best friend, but still . . . I just—ARGH! I DON'T KNOW! I'M JUST AN EMOTIONAL THUNDERSTORM!!!

"Sorry, yeah, go ahead, Melissa. No, I don't care. You do whatever you want. Go to the drive-in movie theater with Brad. Good. Fine. Whatever. Do that. No, I'm not mad. NO, I'M NOT LUMPING MAD! GOOD-BYE!"

WHAT THE LUMP?! Melissa is going to the drive-in with Brad? Like, what lumping YEAR IS IT?!? Who goes to the drive-in?!? Melissa doesn't even like movies; she likes daytime dramas! She totally, like, changes when she's with Brad.

Ugh. Anyway. SIDETRACKED! Now my lumps are grumps. So, that's IT! NO MORE writing today!

I'll just sum everything up real quick and say yes, my life is totes glamsville. You should probably be a lot more like me, and I'm dying a little on the inside because I know you never will be.

Okay, that's it. That's the excerpt. That's ALL you get without buying the whole book.

Peace out, loves!
BUMPS!
THE END!

Buy my book, or I will BITE you and give you the major LUMPS. So, BUY my lumping awesome book already, OKAY?!

FINN AND JAKE'S JUST-FOR-FUN, ONLY-FOR-PRACTICE VILLAIN-VANQUISHING GAUNTLET

Finn and Jake had just gotten *whupped*. They were slowly making their way back through the Cotton Candy Forest. Finn's cheeks were bright

pink and scuffed up, and Jake's butt was in a world of rubbery hurt. In short, they did *not* look so hot.

"Those goblins really stomped on our brains," Finn said.

"Majorly," Jake said. "I'm off my game, dude."

"Hey," Finn said, stopping to look at Jake with all sorts of utmost seriousness. "Don't you say that, Jake. You are just as awesome as ever."

"Your support means the universe to me, bro," Jake said. "And I sincerely appreciate it. But, man, look at us!"

They were standing near a pond, so Finn and Jake stepped over and looked down at their reflections. Staring back at them were, indeed, two *really* beat-up versions of Finn and Jake.

"Convenient pond," Jake said.

In fact, they were *so* beat-up that a turtle even popped its head up and said, "What happened? Did you guys fall off a cliff and land in a pile of punching fists or something?"

"You shut your butt, turtle!" Jake shouted.

"Maybe you're right," Finn said to Jake as they continued walking. "Maybe we *are* off our game."

"Wait, I think it's *games*," Jake said. "Plural. 'Cause it's two of us, and together we're, like, off our *collective* games."

"No way," Finn said. "Game. Single. 'Cause I only know one single game—and that game is *Adventuring and Slaying Anything That's Evil*!"

Jake rubbed his chin. "Um. I don't think that's totally accurate, dude. What about *Wizard Wars*? And *Adventure Masters*? And *Guardians of Sunshine*? And *Conversation Parade*?"

"Oh yeah," Finn replied. "Good point. I guess I do know other games. But I'm not *off* of any of *those* games!"

"Right," Jake said. "Just the important one—the evil-slayin' game! I think we need practice."

Finn thought about this for a moment and then said, "You know what? I think you're right. But that's okay! Even the most radical of heroes need to practice every now and then. So, Jake, . . . WHAT TIME IS IT?"

Jake shrugged. "Um. Like, a little before noon, probably."

Finn stopped and put his hands squarely on his hips. "No, dude."

"Oh right. Sorry," Jake muttered. "My noggin is still sort of scrambled from that goblin beating. Stupid goblins. It's . . ."

"PRACTICE TIME!"

How can two mighty heroes like Jake and Finn get their practice on? Slaying evil is a real-world thing and most definitely not easy to replicate in a rehearsal-type atmosphere.

But Finn and Jake are smart fellas, and they

came up with a supershrew solution. It was . . .

Dun dun dun . . .

FINN AND JAKE'S JUST-FOR-FUN, ONLY-FOR-PRACTICE VILLAIN-VANQUISHING GAUNTLET!!!

A few hours later, the gauntlet was nearly complete. And it was a sick-awesome gauntlet. Finn and Jake built wooden targets of each of their many enemies. When they finished, wooden targets were lining the field in front of their Tree Fort—perfect to test Finn and Jake's evil-defeating moves.

There were a whole freaking *fartload* of wooden villains, including Ricardio the Heart Guy, Tree Witch, Bucket Knight, Hunson Abadeer, Sir Slicer, Marceline's annoying ghost friends, Me-Mow, the Lich, and (last but not least) the Ice King.

Jake and Finn looked out at their *just-for-fun, only-for-practice villain-vanquishing gauntlet!!!*, feeling pretty darn proud of themselves. "Dude, those jerks look pretty real," Jake said.

"Totally. This is gonna be the best practice EVER!" Finn exclaimed.

The Ice King was hiding behind a rock, spying on Finn and Jake. The Ice King had planned on just peeking in on Finn and Jake for a moment and doing a little research for his fan fiction, but now he was intrigued. Because he was looking at something quite odd . . . he was looking at what, to his eyes, appeared to be a great gathering of villains from across the Land of Ooo and beyond!

"What is this?" the Ice King exclaimed. He looked down at Gunter, who offered no help, saying only, "Wak."

"Gunter, it looks like all those villains are having a meet-up."

"Wak."

"They're being a bunch of chatty cathies and trading war stories and swapping recipes without me," the Ice King said, frowning.

"Wak."

"Argh. C'mon, Gunter. Let's get closer," the Ice King said. "We can hide behind that handsome fella at the end there."

That "handsome fella at the end there," of course, was the wooden target of the Ice King. But the Ice King, overwhelmed by envy and a driving desire to swap recipes, didn't even notice. Instead he just crept down the hill, parked his rear end behind the wooden target, and waited, hoping to catch some good gossip before revealing himself.

MEANWHILE . . .

Finn said to Jake, "When we're done running through this practice course, we will totes be ready to crush *whatever* comes our way!"

"Amen, bro!" Jake said.

"All right, you wooden butts!" Finn yelled at the targets. "Prepare to get kicked by non-wooden Finn!"

And Finn was off, punching, kicking, slicing, stabbing, and chopping his way through the gauntlet.

"Heart! Attack!" Finn yelled, slamming a massive kick into Ricardio the Heart Guy and shattering the target *like whoa.*

"Hey, Tree Witch, my sword moves are *off the broom handle*!" Finn yelled as he gashed open the Tree Witch target.

"Sir Slicer," Finn yelled as he held up his hand in perfect karate-chopping form, "meet *Sir Dicer*!

"Me-Mow? NO! *Me-Pow*!!!" Finn shouted as he flicked the Me-Mow target way off into the sunset.

MEANWHILE . . .

The Ice King was in superspy mode. He peered around the wooden target,

still completely unaware he was hiding behind a target of himself.

And what he saw blew his frozen mind! He saw a whole torrent of crazy kung fu Finn the adventurer practice action! He even saw Finn karate chop—*KA-POW*—one villain completely in half!

"Oh my. This is so horrible and gruesome!" Ice King said. "Finn just murdered a guy! That little human seems to have changed his approach to fighting evil."

The Ice King ducked back behind the target of himself. "Oh no. If Finn's murdering villains, that means I'm next!"

BACK TO THE ACTION!!!

"Your daughter," Finn cried out as he rained down kicks on the Hunson Abadeer target, "is so remarkably rad that I *almost* feel bad sneaker stomping you like this!

"I'm legendary for putting Liches . . . ," Finn said, swinging his sword and chopping off the Lich's wooden head, "*in stiches!*"

Finn landed and rolled. When he stood, he saw a wasteland of defeated wooden villains. And now only one target remained.

The Ice King.

"I think," Finn yelled, raising his sword, "it's time to put you *on ice!*"

And with that, Finn spun, ducked, and came up swinging at the wooden target of the Ice King. But Finn—who was used to the ice bolt–blasting, Fridjitzu master, real-life version of the Ice King—was thrown off by how *easy* it was. So when Finn swung, he totally whiffed and went sprawling into the grass!

"Hey, dude, you just whiffed like a big lame-o," Jake said. "But don't worry, I'll handle this one."

Jake's foot began a windup motion, building up power and power and more power, and then—*BAM!*—he unleashed a long, rubbery, *turbo-power kick* at the wooden Ice King.

"*KA-KRUNCH!!*" Jake's foot said—'cause Jake's foot is AWESOME, and if it could talk, it would say things like *KA-KRUNCH!!*—and his foot flew right *through* the Ice King target and into the *real* Ice King, who was still cowering on the other side.

"*KA-POW!!!*" Jake's foot said as it nailed the Ice King right in his big blue belly. Jake's foot was clearly feeling pretty talkative.

"What the what?" Finn exclaimed. "It's the REAL Ice King!"

"Get away, get away!" the Ice King shouted. "You're not heroes! You're horrible and vicious killers!"

And then he ran like crazy back to the Ice Kingdom, moving in the stupid, goofy way an injured, gut-kicked little Ice King does. Finn and Jake had big stupid grins on their faces as they watched him go.

"You know what I think?" Jake said.

"What?" Finn asked.

"I think we are back on our game, dude!"

FIST BUMP!!!

Oh yeah, and then Jake also said, "And, dude, I think your action fatality puns need a little work . . . 'Liches in stiches'? C'mon now."

THE END!

THE TROUBLE WITH GUNTERS

The Ice King held *it* up to the light. *It* was small and pink, and it had taken the Ice King *forever* to get. *It* was . . .

A single piece of magical potionlicious bubblegum!

"Oh yes," the Ice King said, laughing wickedly. "This magical potionlicious bubblegum will allow me to blow the biggest bubblegum bubble in history! I won't need to kidnap Princess

Bubblegum . . . she'll keel over right on the spot. Keel over *with desire*!

"Right, Gunter?" the Ice King said to the penguin closest to him.

"Wak."

"Exactly!" the Ice King said, giggling wildly. "Just need to throw on a few dabs of Randy Glacier cologne, so I'm prepared when the princess lovin' begins."

The Ice King very carefully and very delicately set the magical potionlicious bubblegum piece down on the arm of his ice throne and disappeared into the bathroom.

Moments later, he came back, covered in the confident stink of love anticipation.

"And now it's time for—hey . . . HEY. *HEY!* Where'd my magical potionlicious bubblegum go?" the Ice King said, confused.

It was gone!

Panic-stricken, the Ice King spun about, looking everywhere. Then his eyes locked on *them.* All his many penguins—each of them lovingly named Gunter. And they all stared back at him with their big dumb penguin eyes.

"Gunters . . . did you do something with Daddy's magical potionlicious bubblegum?"

The Gunters stayed silent.

"Did you swallow my magical potionlicious bubblegum?" the Ice King shouted, pointing a long bony finger at the closest penguin.

"Wak," Gunter replied.

"Was it you, Gunter?" the Ice King said, kneeling down in front of one Gunter. "Are you mad because I use you like a TV stand when I play video games?"

"Wak."

"Or maybe it was you, Gunter?" the Ice King said, picking up a different penguin. "Are you still sore over that little comment about your weight? That I called you Daddy's Little Fatty? Eh?"

"Wak."

"Argh! You—you—
you—Gunters!!!!"

"Wak," some other
Gunters replied.

The Ice King collapsed
into his icy throne and
put his head in his hands.
"Do you know what I went
through to get that magical
potionlicious bubblegum?
Do you have any idea of
the horrible, awful things I
had to do? Well, I won't go
into details, but let's just

say—I mean—*bad* things . . . I still feel unclean."

All of the many penguins continued to stare at
the Ice King with their deceivingly cute penguin
eyes.

For a long while, the Ice King sat on his throne, thinking. How could he determine which penguin had stolen his gum? *I'm smart*, the Ice King thought. *I should be able to figure this out. I know! I'll send them all on a trip! A* guilt *trip* . . .

The Ice King kneeled down, talked very softly and sweetly, and pretended to be very sad—which was not that tough because the Ice King is a generally glum and gloomy guy. "Gunter. *Gunters.* My many, many Gunters," the Ice King began. "I've given you a home . . . you many Gunters have become my army. My army . . . of friends. My army of best friends . . ."

The Ice King then quickly followed that up with, "Not counting Finn and Jake."[1]

"Well, my best friends," the Ice King continued, "I really, truly hope you can find it in your cold

---

1. Finn and Jake would totally NOT agree with that, BTW—I asked them, trust me.

penguin hearts to return my piece of magical potionlicious bubblegum. I'm going to turn around now and count to three. I don't even care who took it as long as it's returned."

The Ice King turned his back and began counting.

"One . . .

"Two . . .

"Three . . ."

And when he turned back, there was still no magical potionlicious bubblegum.

"Argh!" the Ice King bellowed.

He grabbed the nearest Gunter, held it upside down, and shook it furiously. "Come out, come out, come out!" the Ice King said as he shook Gunter after Gunter after Gunter.

But no magic gum was revealed.

The Ice King huffed off into the corner. "Use

your brain, guy. You're a king. What would Finn and Jake do? They'd probably say something hip and ironic like *trigonomical* or *scientific*! They're so *cool* and *hip* with their math—"

And the Ice King stopped cold.

"Wait—*math*!"

Suddenly, with furious speed, the Ice King got to work. His hands moved in flashes, manipulating the H_2O particles in the air—he was forming, building, and constructing like an ice *boss*.

After a moment, he stepped back to admire his work. In the center of his throne room now stood a large scale made purely of ice. Icy weighing pans hung from a long beam of ice.

"Now, you stupid identical penguins, I'll weigh you each against one another. And one of you Gunters will weigh more! And *that* will be the Gunter that has swallowed my gum! Oh boy, I'm brilliant," the Ice King continued, giggling softly. "I wish someone was here to see this."

The Ice King began placing Gunters on the scale. "That's it, on the scale. You're next," the Ice King said as he helped one penguin up and into the left pan and another into the right.

"Four point six pounds," he said, reading the scale. "Yes. Okay. Next. Four point six pounds as well, I see.

"Okay, you two pass the test. *For now* . . ." the Ice King said, glaring at them.

The Ice King brought two more Gunters up onto the scale. But, immediately, the Gunter on the right pan began doing a little booty-shake dance.

"Gunter, stop dancing!" the Ice King shouted. "Stop dancing, Gunter! You're muddling the measurements!"

But Gunter ignored him and only began to dance more awesomely.

Then the Ice King *snapped*, like a frozen Slim Jim. He had never been so angry. His blood—usually steady at a temperature of 30°C—began (relatively) boiling. He saw visions. Ice King visions. Horrible, terrifying images danced across his eyes.

"That's it, you prancing Gunter!" he screamed, and then—

KA-SHOOM!!!

Ice bolts hurtled from the Ice King's fingertips!

"WAK!" Gunter scrawked (that's a screech and a squawk at the same time, BTW).

Gunter twirled and booty danced off the side of the pan, just as an ice bolt shot past him. The ice bolt blasted into the ice scale. *KRA-KRUNCH!* There was a big ice 'splosion, and the scale was destroyed, scattering little ice cubes of justice on the floor.

The Ice King was in a frenzied rage. "One of you will spit out my magical potionlicious bubblegum right this second, or I'll send all of you away on an iceberg. One hundred stupid Gunters floating away at sea!"

He got down on one knee and grabbed the closest Gunter.

"Now . . . SPIT. IT. OUT!"

And—finally—that Gunter gave the Ice King what he wanted . . . sort of. Gunter blew a giant magical potionlicious bubblegum bubble right in the Ice King's face.

The gum was indeed enchanted, and it certainly would have allowed the Ice King to blow the biggest bubble ever. Gunter's bubblegum bubble grew bigger and bigger and bigger *until* . . .

POP!!!

The giant bubblegum bubble exploded in a blast of messy pinkness. Sticky, stringy strands of gummy goo coated the Ice King's white beard and white hair and white eyebrows.

"Oh, Gunters . . ." The Ice King sighed.

SOME TIME LATER . . .

Finn and Jake were in the middle of a game of *Portender Defender* when there was a loud knock at the door. Finn hit Pause and walked to the door.

"Jake, you better not un-pause it and double reverse suplex me while I'm answering the door, or I will come back and fart knock you!"

Finn opened the front door. There stood the Ice King, covered head to toe in bright pink bubblegum. "Holy shmow!" Finn said. "What happened to you?"

"Finn?" the Ice King said with a gentle softness. "We're friends, right?"

Finn thought for a moment. "Um. Kinda . . ."

"Well, 'kinda friends' sometimes give each other emergency haircuts, right? To get out stuff? Like, maybe, for example, bubblegum . . ."

Finn sighed. "Come in, Ice King. I'll go get my sword . . ."

"Couldn't you just have had Gunter help with this?" Finn asked.

"*BLERG!!!!*"

THE END!

TREE FORT
FRONT YARD SALE

Finn and Jake were playing Twister, and Finn was *not* having fun. Finn didn't dislike Twister, per se—in fact, he sort of kind of *really* wanted to play Twister with Flame Princess. But Finn *hated* playing Twister with Jake, because Jake never, ever lost.

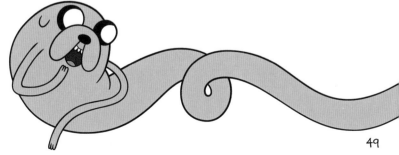

"Left butt, red," BMO said, in that impossibly soft and cute little BMO voice.

"Dude," Finn said, sweat pouring off him as he tried to get his butt over to red. "This—*oww*—isn't really—*argh*—fair."

"Why not?" Jake said.

"You're wrapped around every which way! You've got, like, five elbows and six butts right now!"

"Don't be a hater," Jake replied.

Finn stretched and struggled and reached and moaned and groaned and then—

"*GAH!*"

Finn lost his balance and collapsed on the floor in a sprawled-out human boy heap. As he did, his right foot slammed into the wall of the Tree Fort. And on that wall hung something very sharp and very bright and very poke-y . . .

A yellow dagger.

Finn's accidental kick knocked it free, so that it was now plummeting to the ground!

THUNK!

"Whoa!" Jake said. "I almost got pincushioned! *That is it!* There is an overload of junk in this joint."

"Junk?" Finn said. "What junk? I only see awesome lame treasures."

"Yeah, well, one man's treasure is another dog's junk—and this dog thinks this stuff is junk," Jake replied. "But don't worry. I have a solution."

Finn waited.

"One word . . . ," Jake said.

Finn's eyes were wide with anticipation.

"Tree Fort Front Yard Sale!" Jake exclaimed.

Finn thought for a moment and then said, "That is not one word. That is five words that separately are all kinda *eh, whatever*—although *fort* is pretty much cool no matter what—but you put those five words together, and you know what, Jake?"

"What, Finn?"

"I LOVE it! I am freaking *all about* offering people the chance to buy our radical possessions at bargain-basement prices."

Jake and Finn were going through the tree house, room by room, throwing stuff in For Sale boxes. They already had two big boxes filled to the brim.

But as Finn went through the bedroom, throwing in skulls and helmets and other items, he began to feel a little sad. "I'm maybe rethinking this, Jake. These items hold so many memories . . ."

"Memories I would have *lost permanently*, if that golden dagger of yours had throttled my skull like it almost did," Jake said.

"I guess . . . ," Finn said.

"To put on a good Tree Fort Front Yard Sale, you have to be merciless and cold-blooded, dude. No emotions," Jake said. "Like me!"

"Okay, I guess you're right," Finn said as he tossed an empty cardboard toilet paper tube into the For Sale box.

"NOOO!!!" Jake cried out. "Not that! Whatsa matter with you? That's got memory attached to it."

Jake yanked the empty cardboard toilet paper tube out of the box. "I said 'cold-blooded,' Finn. Not downright heartless."

But pretty soon, they had agreed on a fair number of things which they felt didn't have *too many* memories attached to them. In the front yard, they set up tables. Tables teeming with Tree Fort junk: shark jaws and pelts from strange beasts from across the Land of Ooo and gauntlets and swords and maces and blades and a pillow.

"Hmm," Finn said, looking at the tables. "Do you think we should be selling all these maces and clubs and swords? Shouldn't there be, like, a waiting period or something?"

"Eh, who cares," Jake said. "But you know what we should do? We should put out some hors d'oeuvres. Class this thing up. Get people in the spending mood."

"And look at that," Finn said, pointing at folks coming over the hill. "Here they come now."

"Oh man, now I gotta rush on the hors d'oeuvres!" Jake said, sprinting inside.

They came from all over the Land of Ooo. There was Princess Bubblegum and Snorlock (who was now with his female snail companion) and Tree Trunks and Susan Strong and Peppermint Butler and a whole ton of other dudes!

Princess Bubblegum was browsing one table when she came across the flask that once held her Decorpsinator Serum. "Finn!" she exclaimed. "You're selling this? How *could you*?"

"What's the big deal?" Finn shrugged. "It's empty and harmless. It can't decorpsinate anything anymore."

"That's not the point—it's just that—this . . . ," Princess Bubblegum said. "This has sentimental value. This is from one of our first adventures together."

Finn's cheeks went bright pink (his face cheeks, not his butt cheeks—those stayed pale and white). "You're right, PB," Finn said. "I'll put it back inside."

At another table, the Ice King picked up Finn's flute. Finn had once tried to spear the Ice King with it. "Oh, my dear friends, Finn and Jake . . . ," the Ice King said, cradling the flute. "Oh, the memories. I kidnap a princess, they punch me. And around and around and around it goes. The never-ending dance of—"

"Wak!" Gunter squawked.

"Gunter! You interrupted my melancholy sadness! Don't ever interrupt my melancholy sadness!" the Ice King shouted.

Furious at having his emotional journey interrupted, the Ice King hauled off and *punted* Gunter in his tiny penguin rear end, which sent the penguin hurtling through the air—for once, penguins did fly—and put the rocketing penguin on a direct collision course with . . .

Flame Princess.

Flame Princess was, at that very moment, scolding Finn. "Finn! How could you!" she said. She was holding up a chunk of Finn's flame-retardant suit. "You wore this flame-retardant suit the day we met. Don't you remember?"

"Of course, l remember! But it's just a suit . . . what's the big deal?"

Before Flame Princess could explain why it was so important to her, Gunter smacked headfirst into her flaming hot tushie. Flame Princess— still heated from Finn—turned and *roared*. She conjured a fireball and launched it at Gunter. It went a little something like *FA-SHOOM!*

But Gunter danced out of the way, sending the fireball directly at . . .

Marceline.

At that moment, Marceline was peering out from beneath her big wide-brimmed sun hat and holding up Jake's busted viola.

"Jake! What the what? You're selling this?"

Jake shrugged. "It doesn't work good anymore.

I'm going to take some of the moola I'm earning here and spring for a new fancy-pants viola."

"I'm over one thousand years old, so trust me, I know things come and go, yo. But this viola was from our band moment!" Marceline said.

Jake sighed and yanked it away from her. "Fine! I won't sell MY viola just because YOU don't want me to."

Just then, Flame Princess's fireball erupted beneath Marceline's hovering black boots.

"What the devil?" Marceline said, spinning in midair. And in an instant, Marceline was morphing. One second, she was just a cute, mischievous, gothy, punk vamp queen, and the next she was a foul, dark beast with tentacles as black as night stretching and reaching out from her transforming body.

"*Ahhh!*" screamed Starchy.

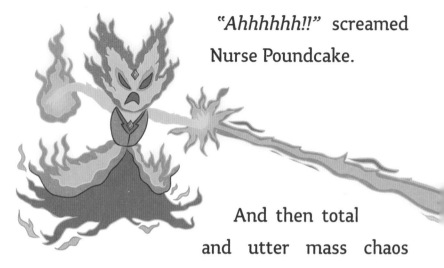

"*Ahhhhhh!!*" screamed Nurse Poundcake.

And then total and utter mass chaos erupted and *everyone* was screaming.

All of this action was quite stressful for Snorlock, who had a tendency to get panicky. His mind totally *freaked out,* and he went on a slo-mo rampage, crashing through the tables, moaning *wewaaahhhhrrrsswe*!

It was a double catastrophe.

When the smoke and ice and flames and slugs and tentacles and checks and everything else cleared, the Tree Fort Front Yard Sale was no more.

It was just a pile of junk scattered everywhere.

Everyone stood around, staring at the mess.

"Wow," Finn said. "That was the most violent Tree Fort Yard Sale *ever*."

Jake stomped his feet. "Dude, that did *not* go well! We didn't make *any* money, and we didn't get rid of any junk!"

But everyone else seemed pretty happy with the way Finn and Jake's Tree Fort Front Yard Sale turned out. Of course, no one had actually *purchased* anything, but the small(ish) calamity that broke out had kept Jake and Finn from selling anything of sentimental value to anyone! Yes! Memories *intact*!

"Also, I don't think anyone liked my hors d'oeuvres," Jake muttered.

THE END!